4   5 billion years ago, our planet, Earth, forms.

3   1 billion years after the Big Bang, the galaxies begin to take shape.

8   2.5 billion years ago, our breathable atmosphere forms.

7   3 billion years ago, life begins with the appearance of the first bacteria and blue algae.

Tyrannosaurus

Argentinosaurus

Baryonyx

Triceratops

Vol. 6

Vol. 5

Vol. 4

Camarasaurus

Scipionyx

Giganotosaurus

Cretaceous

CONTENTS

First published in the United States of America in 2010 by Abbeville Press, 137 Varick Street, New York, NY 10013

First published in Italy in 2010 by Editoriale Jaca Book S.p.A., via Frua 11, 20146 Milano

First edition
10 9 8 7 6 5 4 3 2 1

Library of Congress Cataloging-in-Publication Data
Bacchin, Matteo.
[Mai più così grandi. English]
Giant vs. giant : Argentinosaurus and Giganotosaurus / drawings and story,
Matteo Bacchin ; essays, Marco Signore ; translated from the Italian by
Marguerite Shore. — 1st ed.
  p. cm. — (Dinosaurs)
ISBN 978-0-7892-1013-5 (hardcover : alk. paper)
1. Dinosaurs—Juvenile literature. 2. Paleontology—Cretaceous—Juvenile
literature. I. Signore, Marco. II. Title.
QE861.5.B3313 2010
567.913—dc22
            2010021120

For bulk and premium sales and for text adoption procedures, write to Customer Service Manager, Abbeville Press, 137 Varick Street, New York, NY 10013, or call 1-800-ARTBOOK.

Visit Abbeville Press online at www.abbeville.com.

For the English-language edition: Amy K. Hughes, editor; Ashley Benning, copy editor; Louise Kurtz, production manager; Guenet Abraham, composition; Ada Blazer, cover design.

FOREWORD
By Mark Norell

For most of the history of paleontology (extending back about 150 years), the sauropods were the archetypal dinosaurs: gigantic but boring. They had small heads, long necks, gigantic bodies and long serpentine tails. They were usually represented as dimwitted giants, gray vegetarians that frequented swamps. These dinosaurs were some of the first to be discovered and launched a sort of Bone Rush in the 1870s and '80's as the wealthy patrons of primarily North American museums sent their agents in search of giant skeletons to populate their new dinosaur halls.

Primarily these fossils were found in Jurassic formations of the American west. These dinosaur communities, in which sauropods were the dominant herbivores, were in stark contrast to later North American dinosaur faunas, in which ornithischian dinosaurs like duck bills and horned dinosaurs were the most prevalent plant eaters. The general consensus among paleontologists was that the gigantic sauropods waned in diversity as other hebivorous specialists took their place.

Yet over the last few decades we have found out just how incorrect this picture is. While sauropods may have become less diverse in proto—North America, they flourished in most of the rest of the world. Fossils of sauropods are now known from every continent, their range extending far into the Cretaceous.

And it is not only the cosmopolitan distribution of these animals that is remarkable. They are much more diverse and even weird than previously thought. Some, like *Mamenchisaurus* and *Erketu*, had immense beam-like necks; the Argentine *Dicraeosaurus* had a large frill along the back of its neck; and the African *Nigerasaurus* had a lawnmower sort of mouth with over 500 teeth. Others, like the *Argentinosaurus* in this book, were the largest animals that ever walked on Earth. Along with these giant herbivores came giant carnivores, especially in South America and Africa. Megacarnivores like *Giganotosaurus* and *Carcharadontosaurus* undoubtedly made the world dangerous for even the largest sauropods.

How did these animals live? This is a difficult question for paleobiologists to answer, since we have no terrestrial animals of the same scale to compare them with. Only by making careful inferences from engineering principles can we determine how they held their heads, how much they ate, how they reproduced, how big their internal organs were, whether they were social, or how fast they could move. We have made quite a bit of progess, but there is still an exceptional amount to learn.

DINOSAURS

GIANT VS. GIANT ARGENTINOSAURUS AND GIGANOTOSAURUS

For their help and support both direct and indirect Matteo Bacchin would like to thank (in no particular order) Marco Signore; Luis V. Rey; Francesca Belloni; Sante Bagnoli; Joshua Volpara; and his dear friends Mac, Stefano, Lorenzo M., Giorgio, Donato, Lorenzo R., and Giacinto. But he thanks above all his mother, his father, and Greta, for the unconditional love, support, and feedback that have allowed him to realize this dream.

Marco Signore would like to thank his parents, his family, Marilena, Enrico di Torino, Sara, his Chosen Ones (Claudio, Rino, Vincenzo), Luis V. Rey, Matteo Bacchin, and everybody who has believed in him.

DINOSAURS

Giant vs. Giant

ARGENTINOSAURUS AND GIGANOTOSAURUS

Story and Scientific Drawings
MATTEO BACCHIN

Essays
MARCO SIGNORE

Comics drawn by Chiara Balleello and colored by
N.L.C. Srl–Cinisello B.Mo (MI)

Translated from the Italian
by Marguerite Shore

ABBEVILLE KIDS
A Division of Abbeville Publishing Group
New York London

IN THIS STORY

(Meters)

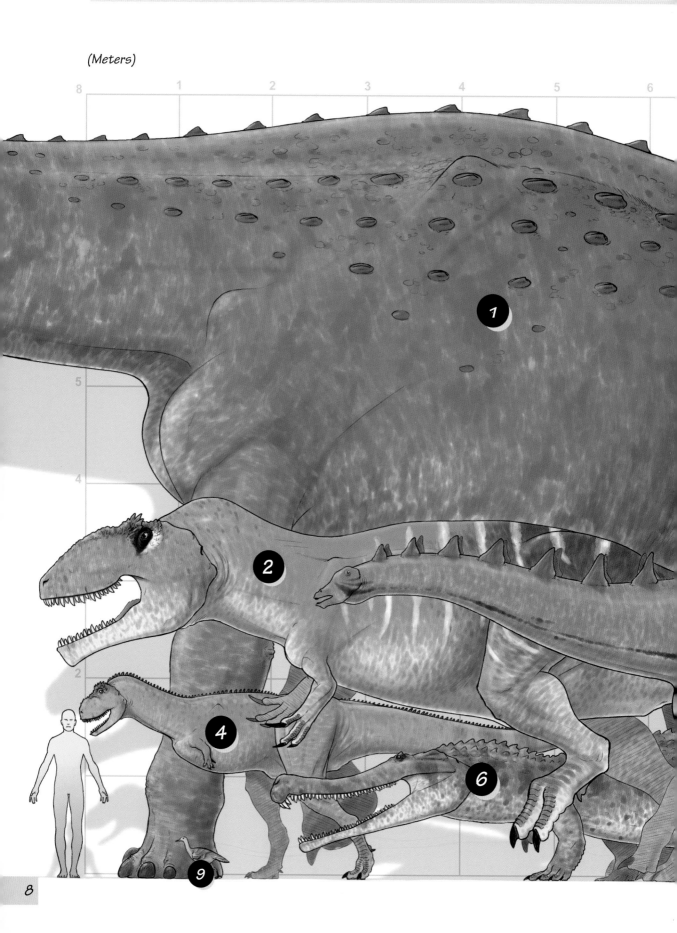

See identikit on page 40

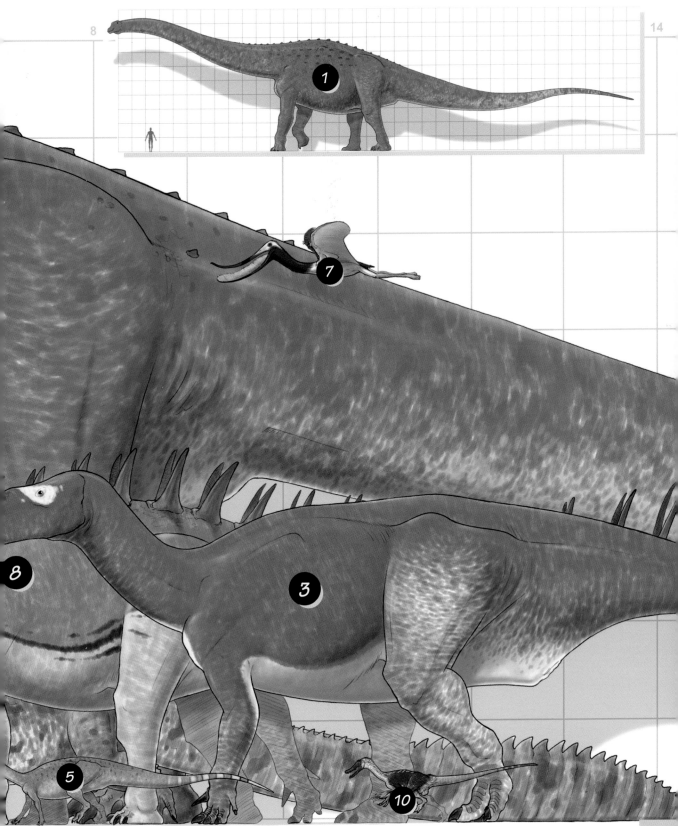

THE NARRATOR

YOU KNOW ME: I AM A SUN. A YELLOW SUN.

ALTHOUGH I AM NEITHER THE MOST POWERFUL NOR THE OLDEST OF MY BRETHREN SUNS AND STARS—ALL BORN FROM THE ETERNAL SPARK OF THE CREATOR-COSMOS—I HAVE SEEN SO MANY THINGS.

MUCH, MUCH MORE THAN MANY OF MY BROTHERS AND SISTERS WHO POPULATE THE SKY AND WHOM YOU CONTEMPLATE ON PEACEFUL SUMMER NIGHTS AS YOU DREAM OF THE FAR REACHES OF SPACE.

IN FACT I AM EXTREMELY FORTUNATE: I AM NOT ALONE IN MY ETERNAL WANDERINGS THROUGH THE SEA OF DARKNESS.

VARIOUS PLANETS HAVE BEEN BORN AROUND ME, AND I HAVE BEEN ABLE TO OBSERVE AND WITNESS MANY DIFFERENT LIVES IN THE TIME GRANTED ME THUS FAR.

I AM GOING TO TELL YOU WHAT I REMEMBER ABOUT PART OF THE LIFE OF ONE OF THESE WORLDS—A SPECIAL AND UNREPEATABLE PERIOD: A MIRACLE OF LIFE THAT EARTH, THE THIRD PLANET AND JEWEL OF MY CROWN, PRODUCED AND RAISED ON ITS FLOURISHING SURFACE.

YOU HUMANS HAVE BEEN ABLE TO DISCOVER LOST MEMORIES OF THIS TIME AS ROCK AMID ROCKS, STONE EVIDENCE BEARING WITNESS TO THAT PAST ERA AND THE RACE THAT LIVED THERE.

THE EONS HAVE TRANSMUTED THEIR ANCIENT BODIES INTO SILENT STONES AND HAVE EMPTIED THEIR CHESTS OF BREATH AND WARMTH.

THEIR EMPTY EYE SOCKETS STILL SEEM TO BE SEARCHING, DELVING INTO YOU AS YOU STUDY THEM IN THE HALLS OF MUSEUMS, HYPNOTIZING YOU WHILE YOU ATTEMPT TO INVESTIGATE, THROUGH THOSE PETRIFIED WINDOWS, THE TWISTS AND TURNS OF THAT PRIMORDIAL ERA.

A DISTANT TIME, WHOSE STORY HAD ALREADY BEEN FORGOTTEN BEFORE THE TIME OF THE PYRAMIDS AND THE SPHINX, BEFORE FIRE, BEFORE THE STONE AGE.

BEFORE THE GODS, BEFORE THE EXISTENCE OF
MAN WAS EVEN IMAGINED, AND EVEN BEFORE
THE MOST ANCIENT MEMORY OF THE WHALES.

A TIME WHEN THESE CREATURES, TAKING
THE WIDEST VARIETY OF FORMS, ABSOLUTELY
DOMINATED THE EARTH.

THEY WERE ABLE TO CONQUER EVERY CORNER
OF THE PLANET, WALKING ITS SURFACE AS NO
RACE BEFORE THEM HAD DONE, EVEN RISING
UP INTO THE SKIES WITH THE HELP OF ONLY
THEIR DELICATE FEATHERS. OTHER SPECIES
MADE WAY FOR THEM; THEY SEEMED
INVINCIBLE. AND YET A MYSTERIOUS FATE
CAUSED THEM TO VANISH.

AND SO ALLOW ME TO CONTINUE THE STORY.

I HAVE TOLD YOU ABOUT THE LONG MARCH
AT THE TIME OF THE NEW TRACKS.

I HAVE TOLD YOU ABOUT THE ERA
OF ASCENT: HOW AN ANCIENT
WINGED CREATURE BECAME
A LEGEND, AND HOW THE
EXPERIENCED LEADER OF
A PACK OF THREE-CLAWED
HUNTERS HAD TO CEDE HIS
PLACE TO A DARING YOUNG RIVAL.

I HAVE TOLD YOU ABOUT AN EGG, A BABY, AND AN
ADULT FROM THE ERA OF THE LAST DINOSAURS.

NOW I WILL TELL YOU ABOUT THE TIME OF THE TITANS
AND SHOW YOU HOW ONE OF THEIR NORMAL DAYS WOULD
SEEM COMPLETELY INCREDIBLE TODAY.

I WILL TELL YOU ABOUT...

THE DINOSAURS

5 GIANT VS. GIANT

DAYTIME, BAD WEATHER.

FOG AND LOW CLOUDS COVER A VAST VALLEY. SOME ARAUCARIA TREES SEEM LOST IN THE HAZE. NOTHING IS MOVING.

BUT WAIT . . . A COLOSSAL SHAPE SLOWLY EMERGES FROM THE FOG, ITS BULK QUICKLY DWARFING THE TREES, THEN ANOTHER AND ANOTHER.

THEY DRAW NEAR ENOUGH FOR US TO SEE CLEARLY: IT'S A PACK OF ARGENTINOSAURS.

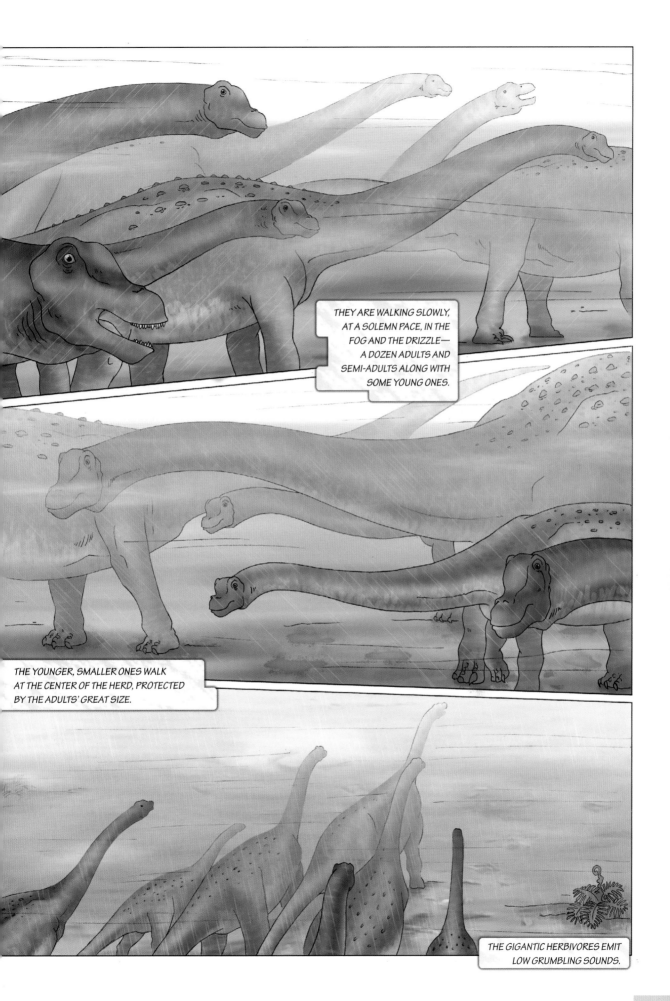

THEY ARE WALKING SLOWLY, AT A SOLEMN PACE, IN THE FOG AND THE DRIZZLE— A DOZEN ADULTS AND SEMI-ADULTS ALONG WITH SOME YOUNG ONES.

THE YOUNGER, SMALLER ONES WALK AT THE CENTER OF THE HERD, PROTECTED BY THE ADULTS' GREAT SIZE.

THE GIGANTIC HERBIVORES EMIT LOW GRUMBLING SOUNDS.

15

NOT FAR OFF, IN THE FOG, A SMALL GROUP OF TREES HIDES OTHER SHAPES.

DIFFERENT SHAPES, ON TWO LEGS.

AS THEY APPROACH, WE CAN SPOT THE JAWS OF A GIGANOTOSAURUS.

HE IS JOINED BY TWO OTHERS OF EQUAL SIZE. THEY DO NOT SEE THEIR PREY, HIDDEN IN FOG, BUT THEY SNIFF THE AIR AND SMELL IT.

THE TWO-LEGGED PREDATORS EMERGE FROM THE GREENERY AND, DESPITE THEIR ENORMOUS SIZE, STEALTHILY APPROACH THE HERBIVORES.

BRAAWW BRAAWW

SNIFF SNIFF

BRAWW BRAAWW

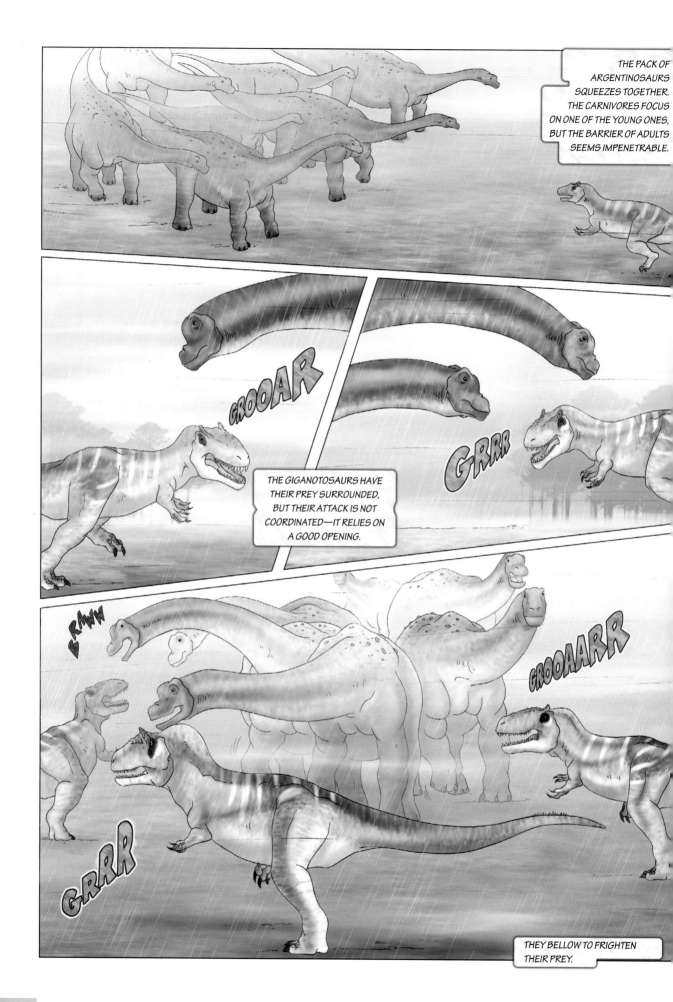

THE PACK OF ARGENTINOSAURS SQUEEZES TOGETHER. THE CARNIVORES FOCUS ON ONE OF THE YOUNG ONES, BUT THE BARRIER OF ADULTS SEEMS IMPENETRABLE.

THE GIGANOTOSAURS HAVE THEIR PREY SURROUNDED, BUT THEIR ATTACK IS NOT COORDINATED—IT RELIES ON A GOOD OPENING.

THEY BELLOW TO FRIGHTEN THEIR PREY.

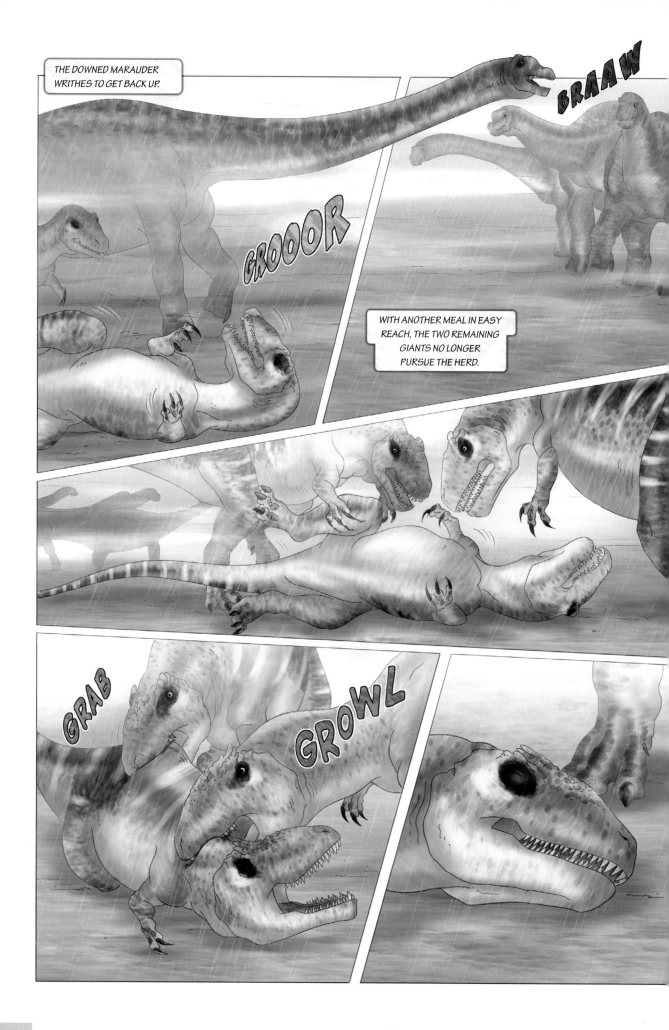

THE PREDATOR BECOMES PREY. ITS COMPANIONS WERE ALLIES BUT NOT FRIENDS, SIMILAR BUT NOT BROTHERS. THEY UNITED ONLY OUT OF NEED.

THE MATRIARCH TRUMPETS; HER HERD MOVES OFF WITH A SENSE OF URGENCY. TAKING ADVANTAGE OF THE SITUATION IS IN THE NATURE OF THE TITANS' ANCIENT LEADER.

THE PLAIN IS NOW FREE OF ITS FOGGY MANTLE.

WITH THE DANGER PAST, THE FAMILY OF TITANS MOVES AHEAD IN A LINE UNDER A LEADEN SKY.

THE MATRIARCH ALWAYS LEADS.

SHE HAS LIVED FOR 100 YEARS AND COULD LIVE ON FOR MANY MORE.

HER ARMORED BACK TOPS A BODY AS BIG AS A PALACE, WITH LEGS LIKE COLUMNS SUPPORTING HER FRUITFUL BELLY.

NOTHING SO LARGE HAD EVER WALKED THE EARTH BEFORE THE TITANS, AND NOTHING SO LARGE WILL DO SO AFTER THEM.

LET'S TAKE LEAVE OF THE ARGENTINOSAURS TO VISIT THE LAKE COMING INTO VIEW.

THE LOW BUT LUSH VEGETATION AROUND IT ATTRACTS A GREAT NUMBER OF ANIMALS.

THERE ARE MANY HERDS OF IGUANODONS, DINOSAURS WITH HORSELIKE HEADS. THEY GRAZE ON THE LOW VEGETATION, WHERE SOME OF THE SHRUBS ARE FLOWERING.

BRAAWW

IT IS MATING SEASON FOR THE IGUANODONS; PANTING MALES WITH SCARLET NOSTRILS RISE UP ON TWO LEGS AND SHOVE EACH OTHER AND BELLOW, TRYING TO ATTRACT AS MANY FEMALES AS POSSIBLE.

SNORT

SNORT

A FEW HUNDRED YARDS AWAY, AT THE EDGES OF THE GROUP, THE YOUNGER AND LESS MASSIVE MALES KICK AT THE DUST, FRUSTRATED AND IGNORED BY THE FEMALES NEARBY.

THE EXCITED IGUANODONS FUME WITH RAGE AT THE ARGENTINOSAURS, WHO SO EASILY PUSH THROUGH THE BUSY HERBIVORES TO REACH THE WATER.

THE LARGE, LONG-NECKED DINOSAURS IGNORE THEM.

BUT MOST OF THE IGUANODONS STEP BACK, AS IF IN A SHOW OF RESPECT.

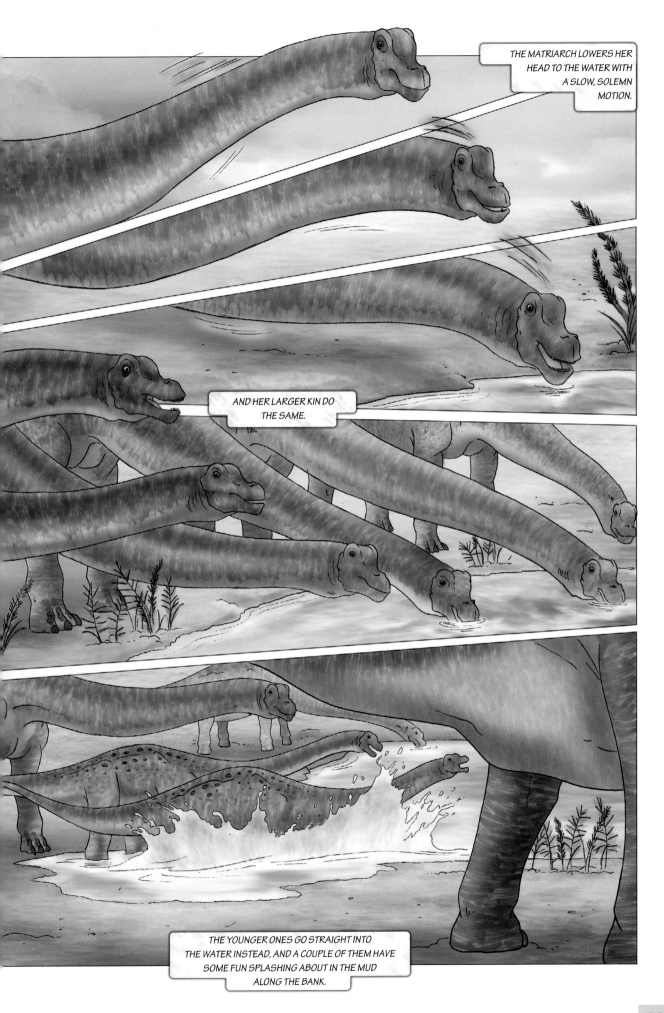

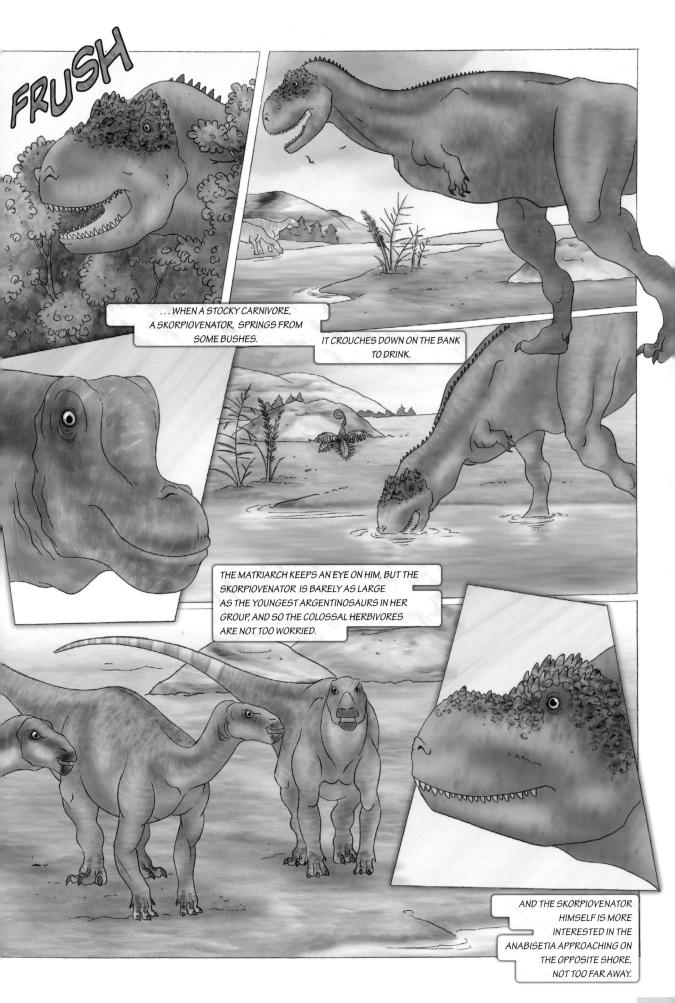

FRUSH

...WHEN A STOCKY CARNIVORE, A SKORPIOVENATOR, SPRINGS FROM SOME BUSHES.

IT CROUCHES DOWN ON THE BANK TO DRINK.

THE MATRIARCH KEEPS AN EYE ON HIM, BUT THE SKORPIOVENATOR IS BARELY AS LARGE AS THE YOUNGEST ARGENTINOSAURS IN HER GROUP, AND SO THE COLOSSAL HERBIVORES ARE NOT TOO WORRIED.

AND THE SKORPIOVENATOR HIMSELF IS MORE INTERESTED IN THE ANABISETIA APPROACHING ON THE OPPOSITE SHORE, NOT TOO FAR AWAY.

THE ANABISETIA ARE NUMEROUS, BUT THEY COME TO THE WATER AS TENTATIVELY AS YOUNG DEER.

THE BRAVEST OF THE HERBIVOR... CAUTIOUSLY APPROACH T... WATER. SOME TREE TRUN... (OR SO THEY SEE... ARE FLOATING ON T... WATER'S SURFA... NOT FAR AW...

THE FIRST ANABISETIA DRINKS; OTHERS IMMEDIATELY FOLLOW.

AN IGUANODON, A SHOWY YOUNG MALE, ALSO APPROACHES.

THEY ALL DRINK LIKE BIRDS, BOBBING THEIR HEADS. MAYBE THIS DISTRACTS THEM, BECAUSE ONE OF THE "TRUNKS" IS APPROACHING . . .

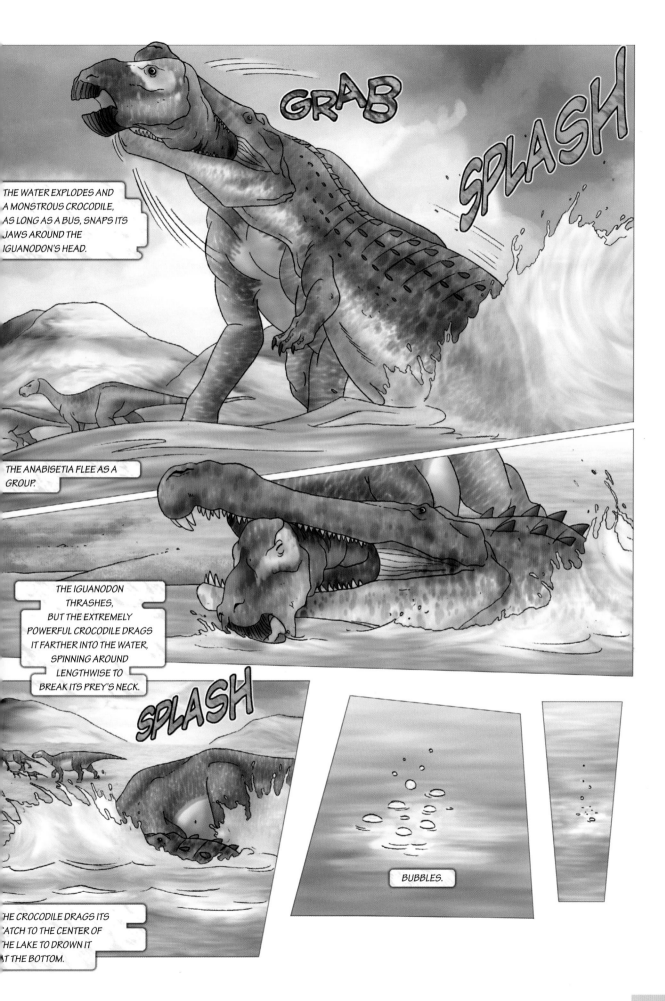

GRAB

SPLASH

THE WATER EXPLODES AND A MONSTROUS CROCODILE, AS LONG AS A BUS, SNAPS ITS JAWS AROUND THE IGUANODON'S HEAD.

THE ANABISETIA FLEE AS A GROUP.

THE IGUANODON THRASHES, BUT THE EXTREMELY POWERFUL CROCODILE DRAGS IT FARTHER INTO THE WATER, SPINNING AROUND LENGTHWISE TO BREAK ITS PREY'S NECK.

SPLASH

BUBBLES.

THE CROCODILE DRAGS ITS CATCH TO THE CENTER OF THE LAKE TO DROWN IT AT THE BOTTOM.

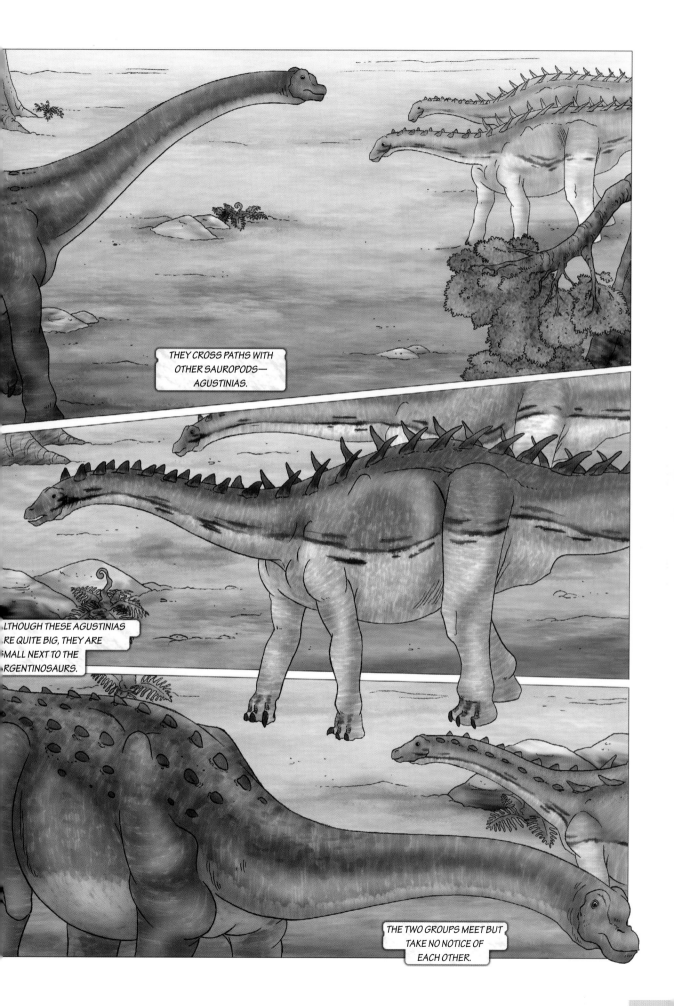

THEY CROSS PATHS WITH OTHER SAUROPODS— AGUSTINIAS.

LTHOUGH THESE AGUSTINIAS RE QUITE BIG, THEY ARE MALL NEXT TO THE RGENTINOSAURS.

THE TWO GROUPS MEET BUT TAKE NO NOTICE OF EACH OTHER.

A GIGANOTOSAUR, WHO HAD BEEN TRAILING THE ARGENTINOSAURS AT A DISTANCE THINKS THE NEWCOMERS WILL BE EASIER PREY

AND DECIDES TO CHANGE DIRECTION.

IT WILL SOON ATTACK.

THE MATRIARCH, SWEEPING PAST SOME BUSHES, HAS FLUSHED OUT A SMALL GROUP OF FLIGHTLESS BIRDS—PATAGOPTERYX.

SOME HOOK-CLAWED DINOSAURS SIMILAR TO VELOCIRAPTORS TAKE ADVANTAGE OF THE SITUATION.

FRUSH

THEY LEAP OUT OF THE TALL GRASS IN PURSUIT OF THE LITTLE BIRDS . . .

. . . ONE OF WHICH ENDS UP BEING SEIZED IN THE FRONT PAWS OF AN AGILE CARNIVORE.

THE SCENE CHANGES AGAIN.
IT IS LATE AFTERNOON—THE SUN IS LOW, AND THE
SHADOWS ARE LONG.

OUR ARGENTINOSAURS HAVE
REACHED THEIR DESTINATION:
A NESTING PLACE.

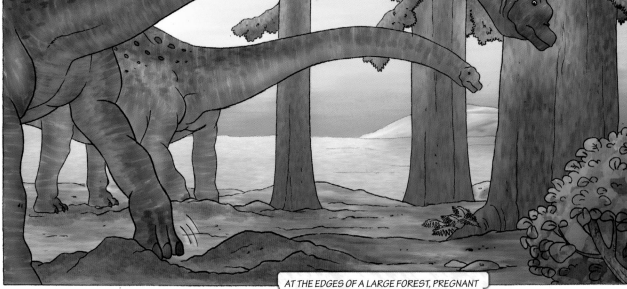

AT THE EDGES OF A LARGE FOREST, PREGNANT
FEMALES DIG THEIR NESTS, USING THE LARGE
CLAWS ON THEIR FEET.

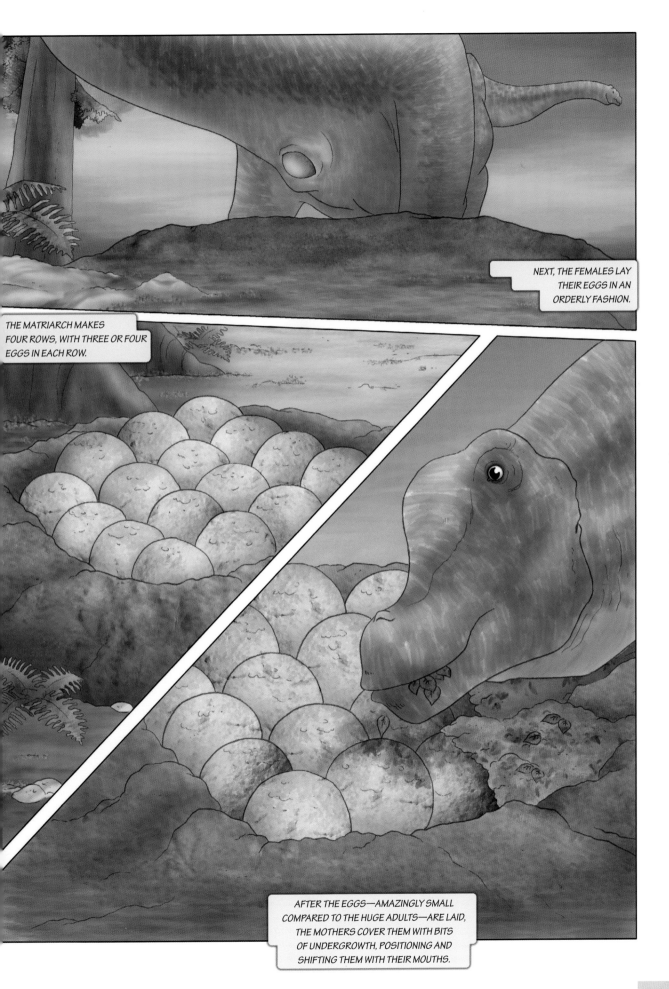

NEXT, THE FEMALES LAY THEIR EGGS IN AN ORDERLY FASHION.

THE MATRIARCH MAKES FOUR ROWS, WITH THREE OR FOUR EGGS IN EACH ROW.

AFTER THE EGGS—AMAZINGLY SMALL COMPARED TO THE HUGE ADULTS—ARE LAID, THE MOTHERS COVER THEM WITH BITS OF UNDERGROWTH, POSITIONING AND SHIFTING THEM WITH THEIR MOUTHS.

BUT EVEN THOUGH THEY LIVE IN FAMILY GROUPS AS ADULTS, THE TITANS—LIKE THEIR ANCESTORS IN THE ERA OF NEW TRACKS—DO NOT TEND THEIR EGGS OR HATCHLINGS, WHO WILL HAVE TO MUDDLE THROUGH THEIR FIRST FEW YEARS ON THEIR OWN.

AND SO THE HERD, NOW THAT IT IS DUSK, ABANDONS THE NESTS AND ONCE AGAIN WALKS OUT TO THE PLAIN AND ITS LAKES.

FAR OFF, A STORM LIGHTS UP THE HORIZON FOR AN INSTANT.

THE LAST GLIMMERS OF DAYLIGHT ILLUMINATE THE COLOSSAL HERD AS IT WALKS MAJESTICALLY INTO THE DISTANCE.

DINOSAUR EVOLUTION

This diagram of the evolution of the dinosaurs (in which the red lines represent evolutionary branches for which there is fossil evidence) shows the two principal groups (the saurischians and ornithischians) and their evolutionary path through time during the Mesozoic. Among the saurischians (to the right), we can see the evolution of the sauropodomorphs, who were all herbivores and were the largest animals ever to walk the earth. Farther to the right, still among the saurischians, we find the theropods. Among the theropods there quite soon emerges a line characterized by rigid tails (Tetanurae), from which, through the maniraptors, birds (Aves) evolve. The ornithischians (to the left), which were all herbivores, have an equally complicated evolutionary history, which begins with the basic *Pisanosaurus* type but soon splits into Thyreophora ("shield bearers," such as ankylosaurs and stegosaurs) on the one hand, and Genasauria ("lizards with cheeks") on the other. The latter in turn evolve into two principal lines: the marginocephalians, which include ceratopsians, and euornithopods, which include the most flourishing herbivores of the Mesozoic, the hadrosaurs.

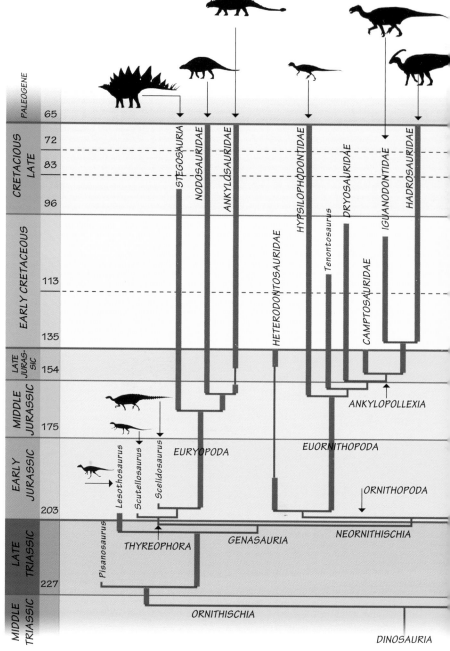

Time (Ma)	Period
65	PALEOGENE
72, 83, 96	CRETACEOUS LATE
113, 135	EARLY CRETACEOUS
154	LATE JURASSIC
175	MIDDLE JURASSIC
203	EARLY JURASSIC
227	LATE TRIASSIC
	MIDDLE TRIASSIC

STEGOSAURIA — NODOSAURIDAE — ANKYLOSAURIDAE — HYPSILOPHODONTIDAE — *Tenontosaurus* — DRYOSAURIDAE — IGUANODONTIDAE — HADROSAURIDAE

HETERODONTOSAURIDAE — CAMPTOSAURIDAE

ANKYLOPOLLEXIA

EURYOPODA — EUORNITHOPODA

Lesothosaurus — *Scutellosaurus* — *Scelidosaurus*

ORNITHOPODA

Pisanosaurus — THYREOPHORA — GENASAURIA — NEORNITHISCHIA

ORNITHISCHIA

DINOSAURIA

IDENTIKIT *(see page 8)*

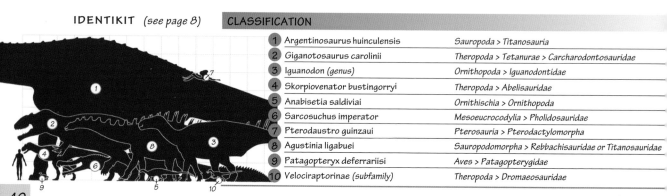

CLASSIFICATION

1	Argentinosaurus huinculensis	*Sauropoda > Titanosauria*
2	Giganotosaurus carolinii	*Theropoda > Tetanurae > Carcharodontosauridae*
3	Iguanodon *(genus)*	*Ornithopoda > Iguanodontidae*
4	Skorpiovenator bustingorryi	*Theropoda > Abelisauridae*
5	Anabisetia saldiviai	*Ornithischia > Ornithopoda*
6	Sarcosuchus imperator	*Mesoeucrocodylia > Pholidosauridae*
7	Pterodaustro guinzaui	*Pterosauria > Pterodactylomorpha*
8	Agustinia ligabuei	*Sauropodomorpha > Rebbachisauridae or Titanosauridae*
9	Patagopteryx deferrariisi	*Aves > Patagopterygidae*
10	Velociraptorinae *(subfamily)*	*Theropoda > Dromaeosauridae*

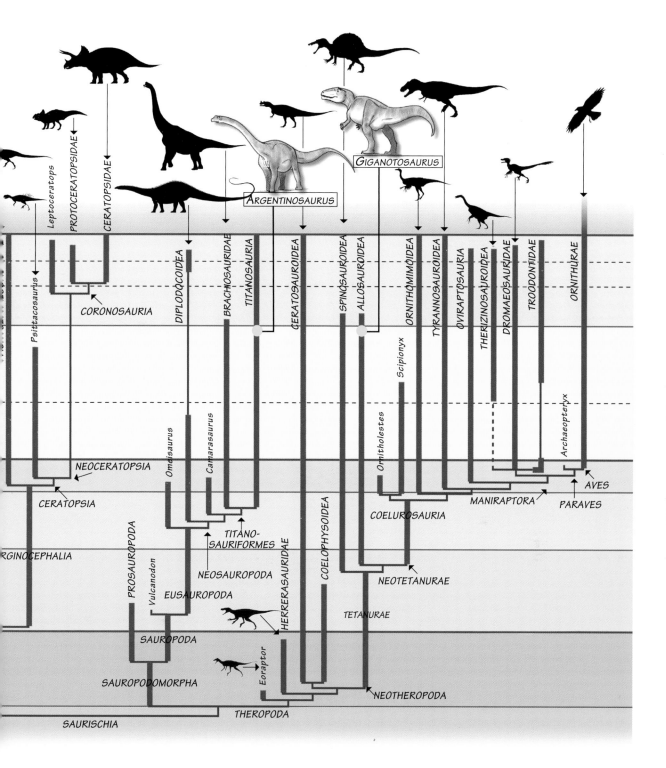

LENGTH	HEIGHT	WEIGHT	DIET TYPE	PERIOD	TERRITORY
over 125 feet	26 feet	80 tons	herbivorous	Late Cretaceous (Cenomanian–Turonian)	Argentina
up to 46 feet	over 11.5 feet	5–7 tons	carnivorous	Late Cretaceous (Cenomanian–Turonian)	Argentina
up to 36 feet	over 10 feet	5 tons	herbivorous	Early Cretaceous (Valanginian–Aptian)	Cosmopolitan
up to 20 feet	up to 6.5 feet	1 ton	carnivorous	Late Cretaceous (Cenomanian–Turonian)	Argentina
7 feet	30 inches (presumed)	44 pounds	herbivorous	Late Cretaceous (Cenomanian–Turonian)	Argentina
up to 39 feet		3 tons	carnivorous	Early Cretaceous (Aptian–Albian)	Africa, South America
wingspan: 6.5 feet			filter feeder	Early Cretaceous (Aptian–Albian)	Argentina
up to 49 feet	over 10 feet		herbivorous	Late Cretaceous (Santonian–Campanian)	Argentina
approx. 20 inches		4–5 pounds	omnivorous or insectivorous	Late Cretaceous (Santonian–Campanian)	Argentina
6.5 feet	20 inches	4.4 pounds	carnivorous	Late Cretaceous	Americas, Asia

THE CRETACEOUS
THE BIGGEST EVER

The Titans of Argentina

▲ A view of the barren territory of the Neuquén Basin, where fossils of the Argentine giants are found.

The arid climate strongly influences the state of the land, subjecting it to strong mechanical erosion.

When we speak about dinosaurs, we normally think of animals from the Cretaceous period, perhaps influenced by the famous book and movie *Jurassic Park*, which, despite its name, presented animals almost entirely from the Cretaceous. After all, the Cretaceous, the last of the three periods of the Mesozoic era, gave us what are perhaps the most incredible and bizarre examples of the gigantic creatures that once dominated our planet. As we saw in our previous book, the Cretaceous was a period of change, when the world moved—both literally and figuratively—to assume the appearance we know today. This period of revolutionary change and wonder was characterized by significant activity in Earth's crust, which shifted, slid, and collided to give shape to a newly configured planet. Gigantic seas opened up and closed again; enormous areas of Earth's surface were submerged by the waters, while vast territories of the ocean floor were pushed upward to form

This is how the skeletons of the giants look during a dig in Argentina. You can see the spinal column and a thighbone of a rebbachisaurid. The bones are freed at the sides, but a support of sediment is left underneath that often is extracted along with the fossil.

Here are the rare remains of an egg. Most finds of fossil eggs consist of shell fragments of varying sizes. Discoveries of entire eggs are extremely infrequent, and eggs that contain fossilized embryos even scarcer.

mountains. It sounds like an apocalyptic scenario, and in fact it must have truly felt like "the end of the world." In some ways the planet was preparing itself for the second greatest catastrophe of all time, as we shall see in our next book.

The characters of our fifth story moved about within this landscape of birth and death, construction and destruction, leaving their tracks on the land that we now call Argentina. These were truly incredible animals, particularly in terms of their size, which would never again be equaled among land animals in the history of life on Earth.

Argentina is a region extremely rich in dinosaur deposits—a true paradise for paleontologists—but its scientific exploration is rather recent. Dinosaur lovers had known for decades about the Argentine sediment layers, principally because fossils from the early history of these great lords of the earth were dug up here. Indeed, the earliest dinosaurs and their direct ancestors were discovered right in Argentina. But more recent expeditions into previously little-known regions in the southern part of the country have yielded incredible results. Deposits have been found containing dinosaur eggs, and remains of animals never seen before have come to light—sauropods larger than any other known dinosaur, theropods of unimaginable shapes—in short, the region is a sort of laboratory of dinosaur evolution.

The Neuquén Basin in Patagonia probably contains the best-known dinosaur deposits in Argentina, and among the finest in all of South America. The evolution of this basin was relatively complex, with the formation of its layers

beginning at the end of the Triassic period. The part that concerns our story is dated to the Late Cretaceous, and scientists recognize in its layers episodes of continental sedimentation associated with marine sedimentation and even volcanic episodes. A review of the dinosaur fauna of the Neuquén Basin has led to interesting developments in both **systematics** (the study of how organisms are interrelated) and **paleobiology** (the biology of fossil organisms), and has even resulted in new and fascinating theories regarding the evolution of dinosaurs in what was the twilight of their reign on earth. But the Neuquén Basin has also yielded vertebrates from the sea, as well as quite interesting marine invertebrates, although both are less famous than the dinosaur fauna.

In the Late Cretaceous, the Neuquén was a retro-arc basin—a sea basin positioned behind an arc of islands, in this case formed from the compression exerted by the shifting movement of the Pacific plates. In essence, Neuquén was squeezed between the Pacific and the rest of South America. This compression caused a **sedimentation thrust of continental origin**. Geologists calculate that the deposits that formed in the principal sedimentation zones are often almost 1¼ miles thick!

However, toward the end of the Cretaceous—and well after our story—episodes of marine transgression occurred, when the ocean began to invade the land due to the global rise in sea levels. This explains the presence of shallow sea deposits, formed after the large continental deposits in which dinosaur fossils are found.

In Argentina there were some dinosaurs that were unique to the southern continent of Gondwana (such as, for example, the abelisaurids), and others that paleontologists consider **cosmopolitan**—that is, living simultaneously on different parts of the planet. It should be mentioned that Gondwana always harbored specialized fauna, and this would continue to be true even after the dinosaur era.

One of the most interesting phenomena for those who study prehistoric fauna is the convergence in development among animals belonging to separate groups, that is, how very different animals, living in different hemispheres, evolved to have the same appearance and cover similar ecological niches. This phenomenon can be seen beginning in the dinosaur era, with animals we have seen in this book, and in the Tertiary it will be equally apparent with the evolution of gigantic mammals that have no family connections elsewhere on the planet, and also with a marked presence of marsupials, which however will decline relatively early on the northern continent of Laurasia. Paleontologists are still not clear about the reasons for this phenomenon, other than greater and lesser degrees of geographic isolation, but it is an accepted fact that the convergence of animals between Gondwana and Laurasia is clearly visible as early as the dinosaur era.

Sauropods

The protagonist of our story is one of the most exceptional sauropods ever studied. Its name is *Argentinosaurus* *1, and it was an animal with columnlike legs and a massive body that could reach the incredible length of 125 feet or more. *Argentinosaurus* means "Argentina lizard," referring to the nation where it was discovered (while the name *Argentina* itself derives from the Latin word for silver, "argentum"). Our knowledge about this creature comes from incomplete remains, and its size may be different from the dimensions calculated by paleontologists. The largest reconstructed skeleton of this dinosaur that we have at the moment, on display in a museum in Atlanta, Georgia, is 121 feet long and represents the largest skeleton ever reconstructed in a museum, at least thus far. So it is no accident that the group that includes *Argentinosaurus* and all the sauropods related to it takes the name Titanosauria

▲ An abelisaurid skull. Note the enormous antorbital fenestra—an opening in front of the eye socket—and the peculiar upward curvature of the jaw.

▶ A paleontologist at work in the flat, dry Argentine terrain.

*1
page 15
panel 1

*2
page 24
panel 2

*3
page 33
panel 1

▶ Another angle on our rebbachisaurid's spinal column. The vertebrae have been preserved in anatomical connection, that is, in the position they occupied in life and maintaining the same relations between adjacent bones.

("titan lizards"), referring to a race of immortal giants who attempted to scale Mt. Olympus in Greek mythology.

Argentinosaurus, like all sauropods, most likely lived in herds *2, and we can barely imagine the impact that a group of these giants might have had on the surrounding environment *3. This dinosaur "titan," however, was not the only giant in Argentina.

Another rather special sauropod that plays a role in our story is Agustinia *4, a truly unusual animal; although it is known only through fragmentary remains, Agustinia immediately claimed paleontological headlines because it was an armored herbivore *5. In fact, the remains that have been discovered include nine plates or spikes that must have been attached to vertebrae, telling us that in addition to their mass, sauropods

▲ The skeleton of the giant, as seen when mounted in a museum. The fact that many bones have been reconstructed does not prevent the skeleton from communicating a sense of power and majesty.

▲ This front limb of an herbivore is disarticulated (that is, the bones are no longer connected), and yet the humerus (at the left) and the radius and ulna (at the right) are still in positions similar to those they would have occupied when the animal was alive.

*4
page 31
panel 2

*5
Page 31
panel 2

must have developed other defensive systems. And they would have needed them: these armored titanosaurids lived in the same environment as the largest theropods ever to appear on earth. Paleontologists are still undecided about the classification of the sauropod *Agustinia* and whether to consider it a member of the Titanosauria family or another family such as Rebbachisauridae. In this book we lean toward this second hypothesis, but the problem still needs to be resolved.

Theropods

Obviously no ecological system in the world is complete without predators, and the dinosaurs of Argentina included many gigantic carnivores. One that stands out is a theropod whose name has made inroads in popular culture: *Giganotosaurus* ✳6, "giant lizard of the south wind." This enormous carnivore belongs to a family of theropods, Carcharodontosauridae, that

was widespread throughout the planet. The long, complex name of this group details the characteristics of these theropods' teeth, which are massive and serrated; in Greek, the word *karcharos* means "serrated" or "sharp," while *odous* means "teeth." It is interesting to note that the great white shark is also called *Carcharodon*, or "serrated teeth," and in fact, the family to which our Argentine theropod belongs was named after this shark, as if to underscore the idea that its innate ferocity was comparable to that of the most notorious marine predator of our own time. Despite a "competition" among various theropods, including tyrannosaurs, animals such as *Giganotosaurus* reigned supreme in terms of size (our theropod is a bit larger than *Tyrannosaurus* and slightly smaller than *Spinosaurus*), almost certainly because of the large size of the prey available to them. Some paleontologists maintain that *Giganotosaurus* hunted the colossal titanosaurs, a hypothesis based in part on the discovery of titanosaur bones in the vicinity of *Giganotosaurus* remains. Other discoveries of groups of numerous skeletons of these predators

▲ A skeleton of the super-predator Giganotosaurus greets visitors to this museum. From our vantage point, it is easy to appreciate the power of this incredible carnivore's jaws.

✳6
page 16
panel 2

✳7
page 18
panel 4

indicate that they may have had a well-developed social life, and perhaps that they hunted in packs *7, thus making this theropod possibly the most dangerous predator in Earth's history.

With their massive dimensions, carcharodontosaurs spread rapidly throughout the world (perhaps in Europe with *Neovenator*, but definitely in North America with *Acrocanthosaurus*, and in Africa with *Carcharodontosaurus*), but in the Late Cretaceous—shortly after our story—they were quickly and definitively replaced by even stranger carnivores called abelisaurs. One of the most primitive animals in this extraordinary group of theropods with truly strange shapes is *Skorpiovenator* *8, an abelisaurid described in 2009 and given its name because the site where it was discovered was swarming with scorpions. An almost complete skeleton of this carnivore was discovered, and it is characterized by, among other things, a quite short snout—a feature that will also be found in other abelisaurids, such as *Carnotaurus*.

*8
page 27
panel 2

*9
page 35
panel 1

*10
page 34
panel 1

*11
page 23
panel 3

*12
page 27
panel 5

▼ *Skorpiovenator, cocooned in a jacket of plaster. In order to extract substantial portions of a skeleton or particularly large bones, paleontologists wrap the find in a rigid jacket, usually made of gauze, or in some cases even toilet paper, soaked in plaster. The find thus becomes much heavier, but this sort of support ensures greater protection when the remains are moved.*

If we consider the full range of carnivorous fauna in Argentina, we find that there were not only super-predators like *Giganotosaurus* and *Skorpiovenator*, but also smaller hunters. In our story there are unspecified small velociraptorines *9, but discoveries in Argentina attest to the presence of other dromeosaurs of considerable size, including one of the latest to be classified, which has very short front legs and is truly a novelty in the field of these medium-size theropods.

And finally, among the theropods we cannot overlook the birds, such as *Patagopteryx* *10, a bird the size of a chicken that had lost the ability to fly.

Ornithischians

Our story includes what is perhaps one of the most famous—and cosmopolitan—dinosaurs among the ornithischians, *Iguanodon* *11. This animal has become part of paleontological legend, in part because it was extremely widespread in the Cretaceous world from Europe to Asia, South America, and Australia, and thus played an important role in the early history of bone hunting. *Iguanodon* was a large animal (over 32 feet long), massive, quadrupedal, and equipped with a sort of spike instead of a thumb claw, which probably constituted this herbivore's sole defensive weapon. Its beak, formed from the predental and premaxillary bones, was slightly dentated in the lower portion, and the teeth, positioned at the back of the mouth, were very similar to those of hadrosaurs, but in their shape recall those of a modern iguana, as the name implies. However, unlike modern iguanas,

Iguanodon was able to chew in the same manner as *Camptosaurus* and the hadrosaurs, which were discussed in the third and fourth books in our series.

Anabisetia ✱12 is also an iguanodontid, but decidedly smaller in size than *Iguanodon*, about seven feet long. Its name is the latinization of the first and last names of a famous Argentine archaeologist, Ana Biset. The *Anabisetia* skeleton is quite well known, thanks to the fact that the four examples identified thus far have various well-preserved bones.

The Late Cretaceous

The last period of the Mesozoic, the Late Cretaceous, was a time of enormous changes.

First of all, the planet changed.

The earth, as we know, is not stable, but in the Late Cretaceous the shifts it underwent became truly "epochal." The continents were literally covered with seas, shallow waters that had invaded the land. The central portion of the United States, for example, was almost entirely taken over by what is called the Western Interior Seaway, a gigantic inland sea populated by incredible animals.

On the oceanic front the situation was less changeable, since Europe and the Americas were increasingly separating, and the Atlantic Ocean was finally assuming its current form. The continent of Laurasia had fragmented, but Gondwana was more resistant in some ways—and this probably explains its specific faunal situation, as we shall soon see.

The climate was cooling, most of all during the final period of the Late Cretaceous, causing a decrease in plant diversity. Animals had to adapt to a world in constant flux, where even the seasons were changing. The tropical climate that had characterized much of Earth seemed to pull back toward what are the tropical zones of the modern world, while elsewhere there began to be a marked difference between the seasons—but we shall discuss this in greater detail in our next tale.

Volcanic activity increased in intensity and was probably one of the causes for the rise in temperatures at the beginning of the Late Cretaceous, which, however, for some reason was followed by an era of global cooling.

To put it briefly, the planet was fragmenting, taking on a conformation more like the world we know today.

The plant world was also evolving. **Angiosperms,** plants with flowers, began their triumphal dissemination, leading to their dominant presence on the planet up to the present day. We can calculate that by the end of the Cretaceous, up to 80 percent of plant species were angiosperms. This, of course, represented a very great change for the animal world, and herbivores had to adapt to a new type of food. Yet despite their rapid diversification and spread, at the beginning of the Late Cretaceous, angiosperms still exhibited little variety, particularly in tree forms, and rather limited anatomical variation. By way of example we can look at the magnolia, which is one of the most primitive angiosperms. Paleobotanists have discovered that angiosperms must have been small plants initially, almost always of an her-

▲ *A present-day magnolia. The magnolia family is almost certainly the oldest flowering plant group, and its members were already widespread in the Cretaceous period.*

✱13
page 27
panel 1

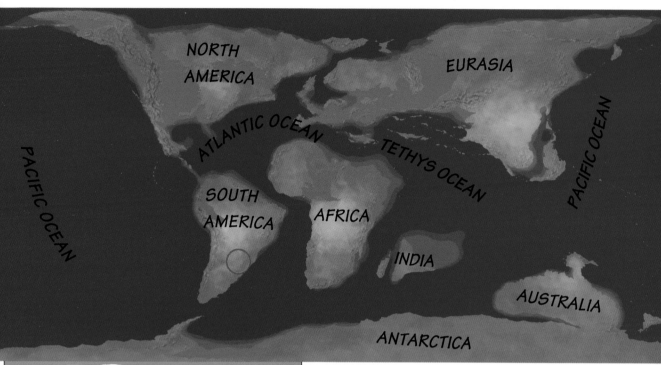

▼ The world as it appeared in the Late Cretaceous. As you can see, the configuration of the continents is similar to how they look today (inset). The exceptions are India, which is still detached from Asia—and whose collision with Asia will cause the Himalayas to rise—and Australia, which is still part of Antarctica and is separated from the other continents. This is why Australian fauna is much more primitive than that in the rest of the world, even to this day. Our story takes place within the area circled in red.

NORTH AMERICA

EURASIA

ATLANTIC OCEAN

PACIFIC OCEAN

TETHYS OCEAN

PACIFIC OCEAN

SOUTH AMERICA

AFRICA

INDIA

AUSTRALIA

ANTARCTICA

GREENLAND

NORTH AMERICA

EUROPE

ASIA

AFRICA

INDIA

SOUTH AMERICA

AUSTRALIA

ANTARCTICA

baceous (or nonwoody) nature *13, or bushes and small trees, that occupied environments subject to rapid modifications, such as zones where new plants quickly replaced one another. Other environments typically colonized by the early angiosperms were salty regions and open forests. Most parts of the forests, however, were still dominated by **conifers *14**, cone-bearing trees like today's pines; their presence, along with the limited dimensions of the angiosperm leaves, indicates a drier climate than one might expect. Large rain forests where vegetation develops literally in levels, from the treetops to the ground, were unknown in the Cretaceous. Another thing we have learned from the study of Cretaceous flora is that the pollination of angiosperms was still primitive in many ways. Most angiosperms depended on the wind and on insects, including bees.

CRETACEOUS	UPPER OR LATE CRETACEOUS	Maastrichtian	72–65 million years ago
		Campanian	83–72 million years ago
		Santonian	87–83 million years ago
		Coniacian	88–87 (85?) million years ago
		Turonian	92–88 million years ago
		Cenomanian	96–92 million years ago
	LOWER OR EARLY CRETACEOUS	Albian	108–96 million years ago
		Aptian	113–108 million years ago
		Barremian	117–113 million years ago
		Hauterivian	123–117 million years ago
		Valanginian	131–123 million years ago
		Berriasian	135–131 million years ago

▲ Stratigraphic division of the Cretaceous. The Upper Cretaceous began with the Cenomanian, and one can see how the levels (that is, the stratigraphic intervals) decrease in duration, because the events are closer in time to us and so we have a greater amount of information. As a result, stratigraphers can isolate geological events with greater precision.

*14
page 23
panel 4

At high latitudes the vegetation was different, with conifers being more plentiful, along with Ginkgoales and Cycadales, while angiosperms diminished appreciably. It is also thought that almost all the plant species present at these latitudes were deciduous (dropping their leaves for part of the year) and grew rapidly during the seasons of extended sunlight and slowed down when the days grew darker (then, as now, there was a sunny season and a darker season closer to the North Pole). Toward the end of the Cretaceous, and principally in the Maastrichtian stage, the climate worsened, and this high-latitude flora became both less productive and less diverse. The number of species decreased, and those that remained experienced less growth. It seems that temperatures dropped beginning in the Santonian or the Campanian stage, and the data that have been collected give the impression that this cooling represented a global event.

Certain fossil sites are particularly interesting for the study of plant communities in the Late Cretaceous, and these include one in North Slope, Alaska, which has presented paleobotanists with a true sequence of plant communities. This site provides much evidence of both global cooling and the aforementioned decrease in floral diversity.

Obviously the fauna of the Late Cretaceous would reflect these changes. First of all, we have the earliest clear evidence of the presence of specific insects, such as butterflies, from the Early Cretaceous. We have already seen that during the final period of the Mesozoic there was an increase in pollinating insects, which adapted to the new plants (angiosperms), and we have evidence of leaf-eating caterpillars, aphids, grasshoppers, and wasps of the Cynipidae family, which produced **galls** on leaves. Hymenopterous insects—bees, wasps, and ants—with their large colonies and complex social organizations, also appeared and began to become diversified in the Late Cretaceous. Early termite and ant fossils have been discovered, as well as fossils of eusocial bees—that is, bees that live in cooperative, specialized hives—tied to the pollination of angiosperms.

Dinosaurs were of course the dominant terrestrial vertebrate fauna, but from the end of the Early Cretaceous we have evidence of a clear differentiation between the animals in the northern and Gondwanian hemispheres. In the northern hemisphere the Early Cretaceous witnessed a decline in the diversity and abundance of sauropods and stegosaurs, while ankylosaurs slowly increased in importance and diversity. But the rapid evolution of the plant world was reflected

◀ Deinonychus *hunting at dusk. In addition to its famous scythelike claw, the use of which we still do not have a clear picture of, one can see the animal's "feathery" covering; Chinese dromeosaurs have been discovered that are completely covered with different types of feathers. We know that* Deinonychus *hunted in packs.*

✳15
page 29
panel 1

among fauna by an equally rapid increase in ornithopods. Animals such as *Iguanodon* became extremely important worldwide, in part thanks to the adaptation of their tooth structures, or dentition—which undoubtedly gave them an advantage from the standpoint of feeding that went beyond the capabilities of any other herbivorous dinosaur of the time. Ceratopsidae was another group of ornithischians that benefited from the ability to consume new plants, and in the Late Cretaceous they would diversify into an incredible variety of forms, generally quite large.

Carnivores, in turn, then necessarily adapted to the new herbivorous fauna, and various evolutionary trends developed in small and medium-size predators (such as dromeosaurs, including *Velociraptor*, and troodontids) on the one hand, and the carnivores of enormous size (tyrannosaurids) on the other. It should be mentioned that spinosaurids and carcharodontosaurids were still the largest, even after the appearance of tyrannosaurs, but they only managed to compete seriously in Gondwana.

In the southern hemisphere, which obviously includes Argentina, the array of animal life was slightly different. Sauropods continued to diversify and to dominate the herbivorous fauna, with the largest titanosaurs predominating. The theropods gave rise to a completely new group

characterized by absolutely bizarre forms: abelisaurids, which would replace the much larger carcharodontosaurids as the dominant predators. However, dromeosaurs also succeeded in diversifying in the southern regions, attaining considerable size and often unusual adaptations, such as a reduction in the length of their front limbs.

But terrestrial fauna clearly did not include only dinosaurs. In the Late Cretaceous mammals were already diversified, and multituberculates, an extinct type of rodentlike mammals, developed arboreal capacities, adapting to life in trees, and thus were able to feed at different levels. Among the reptiles, sphenodonts were still making a comeback, and herbivorous forms were equipped with relatively sophisticated chewing mechanisms for their type.

At this point crocodiles had steadily adapted to aquatic environments, and they evolved into forms of impressive dimensions, such as *Deinosuchus* (whose length has been calculated at more than 52 feet), and *Sarcosuchus* ✳15, seen in our story, which may have exceeded 39 feet. It should be noted that since there are no complete skeletons of these gigantic crocodiles, their length has been

▲ Carnotaurus, *exhibited at a museum in Madrid. This abelisaurid is a truly bizarre animal, with extremely short front legs and a short, rounded snout. Two horns over its eyes give it the appearance of a demon or a bull—from which its name is derived.*

▶ Tupuxuara, *one of the pterosaurs exhibited at the American Museum of Natural History in New York. Like all pterodactyloids, this example also has a large crest on its skull, and it has practically no tail. Many pterodactyloids lack teeth, and this is no exception. Some paleontologists think that Tupuxuara ate fruit, making it a frugivore.*

✳16
page 26
panel 1

calculated for the most part by measuring the skull and then extrapolating the other dimensions based on the proportions of living crocodiles. Such gigantic crocodiles almost surely would have been able to bring down large dinosaurs, seizing them and dragging them into the water, just as their much smaller present-day relatives do with their prey. To give you a better idea of their size, the largest crocodile alive today, the Australian marine crocodile (*Crocodylus porosus*), does not grow longer than 20 feet in length.

In the skies, pterosaurs attained the greatest diversification. The early pterosaurs known as Rhamphorhynchoids completely disappeared, and the skies belonged to the pterodactyls and to the birds. The gigantic azhdarchids, which we shall see in our next volume, could have a wingspan of close to 50 feet, and a recent discovery of some enormous pterosaur tracks hints at animals that might have had a 65-foot wingspan.

But their diversification was not limited to size. The pterosaurs that dominated the Late Cretaceous skies also experienced enormous diversification into various **trophic niches**. *Pterodaustro* ✳16, seen in our story, exemplifies this adaptive search for new food sources. This spectacular South American pterosaur was, in fact, completely lacking in typical teeth and instead had a series of structures similar to the small plates of present-day phoenicopteri (flamingos)

or the baleens of whales. Based on these structures, we can state that *Pterodaustro* fed on microscopic animals, filtering them from the water just as flamingos do. But the adaptations did not end there: pterosaurs began to develop incredible-looking, even excessive, crests. For example, *Nyctosaurus*, a North American animal, which had no claws with the exception of the "thumb" on its hand and probably spent almost its entire life in flight, was equipped with a long, thin crest with an L-shaped branch over four feet long. According to some scholars this crest supported a sort of sail—similar to that used for windsurfing—which would have given the animal aerodynamic advantage.

South America also had other pterosaurs with bizarre crests: the *Tapejara*, short-beaked and almost always toothless, had a crest of truly incredible shape and dimensions.

All these adaptations almost surely mirrored the attempt by pterosaurs to seriously compete with the latest arrivals in the Cretaceous skies, namely birds. In the Late Cretaceous birds were already confirmed fliers, in part thanks to their feathers, which offered clear advantages over the membranous wings of pterosaurs. Moreover, as we have seen in our story, from the beginning of the Late Cretaceous birds also began to adapt to the possibility of living on the ground without flying. *Patagopteryx*, in fact, was a bird that had

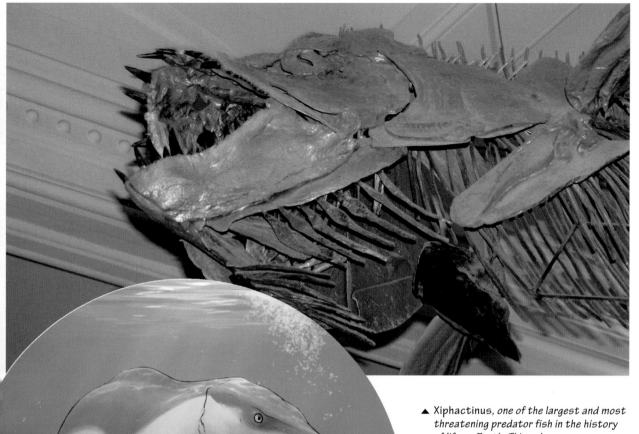

▲ Xiphactinus, *one of the largest and most threatening predator fish in the history of life on Earth. This colossus was over 16 feet long and hunted in the waters of the Western Interior Seaway of North America at the end of the Cretaceous. A pair of its relatives, much smaller, swam in Italian waters.*

◀ *A mosasaur. These aquatic lizards, not related to the plesiosaurs, could grow extremely large. It is very likely that they were super-predators in the Cretaceous seas, more than mere competitors even for large sharks such as* Cretoxyrhina.

obviously come from flying ancestors but had lost its ability to fly. It seems to be on many levels a true herald of the avian domination to come in the Tertiary.

The seas of the Late Cretaceous were not exempt from the great changes of the period. There was a decline in the marine reptiles known as ichthyosaurs, which would become extinct well before the dinosaurs. But this does not mean that there was a lack of marine predators. Some gigantic fish predators appeared, such as *Xiphactinus*, and

toward the end of the Cretaceous they became true threats to the inhabitants of the seas. Fish of this type were probably common in almost all seas, although this "sword ray" (the meaning of the name *Xiphactinus*) was known principally in North America. This fish was able to rapidly swallow its prey, even at risk to its own life, as seen in an exceptional *Xiphactinus* fossil of an individual suffocated by a bite that was too large. And yet despite its size—well over 16 feet long—this gigantic hunter-fish also became prey for the creatures that dominated the Late Cretaceous seas: sharks and mosasaurs. Sharks with more "modern" forms—ancestors of the ones we know today— now ruled the seas. Animals such as *Cretoxyrhina* most closely resembled present-day sharks, and they clearly had an existence similar to that of the modern white shark or tiger shark.

Mosasaurs, on the other hand, have no modern equivalent. These were lizards—probably relatives of present-day monitor lizards—that had adapted perfectly to life in the sea. They were on average about 16 feet long but could exceed 32 feet, in examples such as *Tylosaurus*, and they were very well equipped to be deadly hunters. However, these predators also managed to adapt to other diets: paleontologists have discovered mosasaurs with blunt teeth that enabled them to feed on mollusks with shells; others had snouts shaped like those of crocodiles; and still others had incredible numbers of teeth.

Mollusks were dominant in the world of marine invertebrates. Ammonites and belemnites were at the apex of their evolution, sometimes attaining extraordinary dimensions, as in the case of *Pachydiscus*, a Campanian-era ammonite with a diameter exceeding six feet. It is probably the largest shelled mollusk that has ever existed.

In any case, mollusks were predominant in the **benthos**, and oysters already made up veritable reefs, formed from stacks of their large and often thick shells. Finally, we should mention that foraminifera, microscopic single-celled animals with truly splendid forms, spread rapidly in plankton in the Late Cretaceous.

The Dinosaur Diet

Here, as well as in the earlier volumes, we have discussed both carnivorous and herbivorous dinosaurs, but now we need to clarify one very important aspect of the biology of these great creatures that ruled Earth: their diet.

Our common perception of the animal world is often deceptive, for we generally divide animals into "carnivores" and "herbivores" without going into further detail. On some levels, this clarifies the discussion of the ecology of animals. And yet, as soon as we look more closely at nature, we realize that something is not right about our extremely pared-down, two-part system.

Let's proceed in stages. Among vertebrates it is possible to make a distinction between carnivores and herbivores, primarily by looking at tooth structure. Teeth are the essential characteristic and the principal tool that allows an animal vertebrate to be able to "process" food, that is, work on it, modify it, and make it digestible. When we humans make an omelet, we first break the eggshell and throw that part away rather than adding it into our meal. The action of breaking and throwing away the shell is part of "processing" the food. Animals are able to do this, too, but they normally use their teeth for this purpose.

Thus, in theory, it is possible to look at the tooth structure of a vertebrate in order to understand its *basic* diet—but please keep in mind this word *basic*, because we shall see many, many exceptions to the rule. Things can often become more complicated. For example, mammals have the advantage of being able to count on many different types of teeth in the same mouth. The canines are structured for grasping, the incisors for cutting, and the molars for chewing. Some dinosaurs also had different types of teeth in their mouths, as we shall see when we talk about herbivores.

Although related to diet only in that it helps in acquiring food, another thing that makes it possible to distinguish between "herbivores" and "carnivores," at least among dinosaurs and mammals, is the position of the eyes.

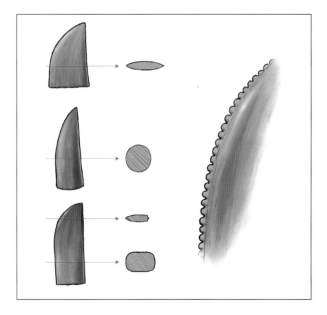

▲ At the upper left is a tooth structured for cutting; at the center, we have one with a circular cross section, adapted for grasping; at the bottom is a four-sided one with a flattened point, adapted to withstand great stress and thus to cut flesh and bone. The detail to the right zooms in on an area of serration; serrated teeth are undoubtedly the best for cutting flesh.

Carnivores

Let's take a look now at the entire mouth of a carnivore. The teeth must be able to cut flesh in order to eat it. But what is the best shape for cutting flesh? The first vertebrate predators, placoderms (animals similar to fish but heavily armored), were endowed with blades instead of teeth, blades that derived from the animal's own armor. These cut food into smaller parts, without precision, just like an axe. And it is no accident that the largest known placoderm, *Dunkleosteus*, had veritable axe blades rather than teeth. This model apparently did not work well, though, because placoderms became extinct well before the middle of the Paleozoic era. The best way to process food is not in fact with a crude blade, but rather with more specialized structures. This is where teeth come into play. Now, if we observe the teeth of a carnivore, we realize that there is not a "single model" that works for all predators. We commonly think that the teeth of meat-eaters must all be pointed and sharp, but you only have to go to a museum to see that in real life things are quite different.

In fact, there are teeth suitable for seizing, others suitable for holding on, others for crushing,

▲ Masiakasaurus, *a peculiar fish-eating dinosaur from Madagascar. Its front teeth formed a sort of basket with which the animal was able to trap fish. Similar adaptations are rare in land animals, but a tooth configuration like this one is found in certain pterosaurs.*

▼ Dunkleosteus, *perhaps the first predator of large size that ever plowed Earth's seas. This is not a modern type of fish, but a placoderm, and its jaws are armed not with teeth but with armor plates as sharp as axes. It must have been one of the most dangerous hunters of its time.*

◀ *Gallimimus, an ornithomimid. Its mouth has no teeth, but we know from some finds that the beak of these dinosaurs was equipped with thin plates similar to those of present-day ducks. Some of them were probably able to eat like modern geese.*

▼ *Shuvuuia, a small dinosaur, probably specialized in hunting social insects, such as ants. The first finger of the hand, equipped with a large claw, may have been used for splitting open the walls of anthills.*

and still others for cutting. What is the reason for such a variety? It is simple: not all prey are alike. When we sit down at the table, we do not always eat the same type of food every day. If we go to a fancy restaurant, we are faced with different types of forks, knives, and spoons, each adapted for one and only one dish. Animals' teeth solve the same problem. For example, those that feed solely on fish do not need blades for cutting or grind-stones for crushing. Because fish are slippery, they need structures suitable for holding on and even piercing. *Masiakasaurus* is perhaps the best example of this among dinosaurs; its teeth were cone-shaped, made for puncturing, not cutting. Other animals, such as many fish, crocodiles, and dolphins, have a similar type of teeth. Animals that feed on fish are often called *piscivores*.

Then there are certain carnivores that prefer to eat food that has very hard parts. We would never think of eating a nut with the shell on, would we? Yet many marine animals, such as rays, feed on mollusks—clams and similar animals protected by hard shells. As a result, while they are carnivo-rous predators, their teeth are made for crushing,

not for slicing. Their flat, robust teeth are perfect for breaking the hard covering of their prey. Thus far, no dinosaurs have been discovered with this sort of tooth structure, but the theropods called oviraptors were long considered valid candidates for a similar diet. One oviraptor was even called *Conchoraptor*, or "shell plunderer." The robust but toothless jaws of oviraptors have led some scien-tists to think that they had a diet based on hard foods, encouraging the belief that these dinosaurs stole eggs (the egg, after all, is a hard-shelled food!). Predators of hard animals are called *durophages*.

The skull of Amphicyon, *a predatory mammal. Its snout has become shorter and stumpier; the teeth have diversified into incisors, canines, and premolars/molars, and thus chewing is "invented." This animal had a powerful bite, which we can establish from the large central crest on the skull and from the height of the mandible, or jawbone.*

✳17
page 16
panel 3

Most theropods were equipped with a specific type of tooth: a flat, serrated blade, a bit like a steak knife ✳**17**. Have you ever tried to eat a steak with a butter knife? Cutting a slice of meat with a butter knife can be quite an undertaking, but using a serrated blade makes the task truly easy! The reason is that every single tooth along the sawlike edge not only cuts but also traps a piece of the food, and thus facilitates the task of the teeth that follow and literally "tear" the fabric. And so it should be no surprise that large predators such as *Tyrannosaurus* and *Giganotosaurus* were equipped with serrated teeth. And, as we discussed earlier, this anatomical feature inspired the name of the great white shark, *Carcharodon carcharias,* whose serrated teeth are perfect cutting tools. Any animal endowed with such teeth, however, can do only one thing: cut. And so, while the animal is able to inflict devastating wounds on its prey, it can only swallow its food in chunks, without breaking it up. In other words, there is nothing subtle about carnivores equipped with serrated bladelike teeth.

In addition to these examples, predators exhibit other adaptations. For instance, the tooth structure of felines is not suitable for cutting, but rather for getting a powerful and stable bite. In fact, cats kill their prey either by breaking its neck with one bite or by grabbing it by the throat and strangling it. Contrary to what is shown in many films, they do not bite open the jugular vein, but literally strangle their prey. Their teeth—and snout—are constructed exclusively for this purpose.

We must also remember that insects are animals, too, and a creature that eats insects is also a predator. Were any dinosaurs insectivores? Probably. Paleontologists who have studied the characteristics of certain dinosaur skeletons have hypothesized that at least three theropods were specialized insectivores: *Shuvuuia, Epidendrosaurus,* and *Epidendripteryx* all exhibit adaptations, above all in their teeth, or lack thereof, that seem perfect for an insect-based, or *entomophagous,* diet.

Finally, we should look at three specific adaptations. The first is *necrophagy,* namely the scavenging and the eating of the bodies of dead animals. With the exception of vultures, no tetrapod (a vertebrate with two pairs of limbs) is exclusively necrophagous, but, as we shall see in our next tale, it is impossible to believe that dinosaurs would have refused to eat a carcass when they found one.

The second adaptation is perhaps the most complex: *omnivory,* or eating a bit of everything. We have seen in previous books that certain theropods have strange teeth or even have no teeth. Think of the ornithomimids. What did these "ostrich-dinosaurs" eat? The most likely answer is that they ate like many present-day birds, such as ostriches or ducks: they essentially consumed anything edible within mouth range. I personally have seen ducks eating fish or even the body of a gull, and it is known that ostriches can consume practically everything. Why, then, should we rule out that some dinosaurs might have had this extremely advantageous type of diet?

The last adaptation is that of *filter feeders*—animals that eat very small food particles that occur in water. Normally, filter feeders are found among marine invertebrates—for example mussels or clams, and many worms—but vertebrates also include filter feeders, and these generally attain colossal dimensions! In fact the largest living vertebrates, baleen whales and plankton-eating sharks such as the whale shark, are filter feeders. They have strongly modified teeth, transformed into hairs, which serve to sift and hold back the plankton from the water. In our story we saw a pterosaur filter feeder, *Pterodaustro*. There were also dinosaur filter feeders, and it is possible that some ornithomimids (such as *Pelecanimimus*, seen in the last story) also fed in this way. All filter-feeding vertebrates eat microscopic animals, and thus they are predators of a sort—and this is why they are included at the end of our brief look at carnivores.

*18
Page 15
panel 1

Herbivores

Herbivores face a very different situation. They generally eat food that is less protein-rich than carnivores, but which has the advantage of not being able to run away. Herbivores are not all alike, however, and in ecology they are divided into many categories: grazers, gatherers, and so on. Accordingly, the tooth structure of herbivores also varies.

We can gather a vast amount of information about herbivory just from dinosaurs. Let us begin with the giants described in our story, the sauropods. The tooth structure of sauropods is commonly thought of as weak and undifferentiated, but any dinosaur lover knows that things are not so simple. Certain sauropods were equipped with small teeth arranged only at the end of the snout *18 (for example *Diplodocus*), while others had robust and more numerous teeth. Why? Simply put, the mode of eating determines the type of teeth. Plants are not all alike. While generally more resistant than meat, they have different degrees of resistance. Try to eat some celery and some zucchini, and you will quickly see these differences. The celery is crunchy, while the zucchini is softer. A nut will be truly complicated to eat without a nutcracker, while berries can be swallowed by the dozen—as long as you are not worried about the stomachache that might result. And so contrary to what one usually thinks, her-

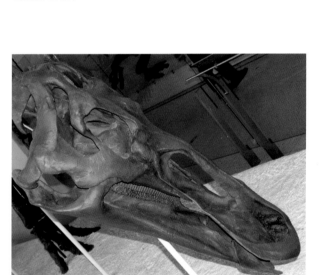

▲ The skull of an Anatotitan, the largest known hadrosaur. Its dentition, in the rear portion of jaws shaped like a duck bill, was made up of hundreds and hundreds of small teeth that functioned as a true grindstone.

▲ Triceratops had a mastication (chewing) mechanism similar to that of Anatotitan and the hadrosaurs, but a bit less sophisticated. The ceratopsian beak was sharp and parrot-like, so these animals were able to eat tougher plants.

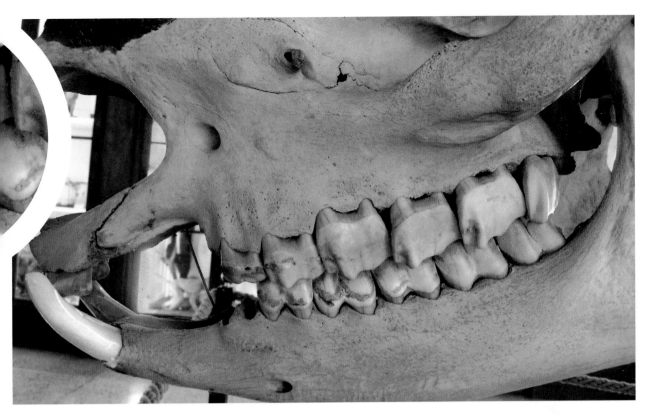

bivores need much more specialized teeth than carnivores.

Let us begin with the simplest form of herbivore: this would be an animal that is limited to collecting leaves and swallowing them, while the stomach takes care of the work of slowly grinding them up. These animals need teeth that we call "nonspecialized," but this term is really not correct because, in fact, their teeth are specialized for gathering. When you serve salad at the dinner table, you use a particular kind of paired utensil to collect it, otherwise you would drop piles of salad all over the table when serving it. Well, these "salad tongs" of the animal world have a tooth structure very similar to our salad servers. Thus, the teeth of *Diplodocus*, small, peg-shaped, and turned forward, act precisely in the same way: for gathering. Why waste metabolic energy forming complex teeth, when it is the stomach that deals with grinding up the food—with the help of some stones, as we have seen in previous volumes? This is why these animals are limited to gathering plants, then later "processing them" at their convenience. Many herbivorous mammals—horses and rhinoceroses, for example—use their incisors in a similar fashion.

However, many plants don't allow themselves to be eaten without putting up a fight, and so they develop defenses like tough leaves and very hard branches that must be cut before being gathered. Human beings use a special tool for cutting

▲ A present-day rhinoceros. Its front teeth (incisors) are structured to collect vegetation, while the premolars and rear molars are massive, with sharp edges (see a close-up of the molars in the inset) for chopping food. Note how this overall structure resembles those of Anatotitan *and* Triceratops, *only instead of incisors, dinosaurs used their beaks.*

grass: the scythe, a blade with a handle, in all its variations. Likewise, many sauropods also had robust and sharp teeth that probably were used for cutting the hardest branches before swallowing them, acting as small scythes, which were extremely useful for eating flexible and leathery food.

Thus the cutting and gathering of plant material is of utmost importance for herbivores. Sauropods, while diverse throughout almost the entire dinosaur era and larger than any other terrestrial animal we know, were still limited to gathering food. In some cases they adapted to doing this from varied heights, as suggested by the different neck types of various groups of sauropods, with some held horizontally and others upright. Most of the work of processing food, however, took place in these giants' stomachs. One paleontologist has defined sauropods as "fermentation tanks with legs"—that is, enormous containers in which plants fermented and were digested, moved about by massive legs and with a collection mechanism . . . what you might call a sort of titanic vacuum cleaner!

But the life of an herbivore was not so simple; size, for example, was a factor.

The Eyes of the Predator

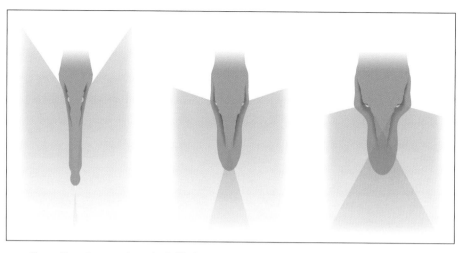

▲ These three images show the field of vision in predators, depending on the position of the eyes. At the left, lateral eyes, placed to the sides, allow a very wide peripheral field of vision (light blue), but a very small binocular field of vision. At the center, eyes in an intermediary position allow better binocular vision (dark blue), but a smaller field of peripheral vision. Finally, the image at the right shows the standard range of an evolved predator; the eyes are turned forward, and the peripheral field of vision is reduced, but the binocular field of vision is very wide.

The problem with plants is that they are often particularly resistant both to chewing and to digestion. Sauropods resorted to swallowing stones to grind their food, and probably had extremely muscular stomachs. Fortunately, the problem of processing plants that were difficult to digest could be resolved in ways other than swallowing dangerous stones, as we shall see in ornithischians. The most obvious solution was to chew food fairly well before it moved on to the stomach compartment.

The innovation of "chewing" food is not the domain solely of mammals, although the latter enjoy the advantage of having an extremely mobile mandible, or jaw, good for mastication, or chewing. In previous books we have already seen the great adaptive step in herbivorous dinosaurs, namely the capacity to chew, with the formation of true sets of teeth that functioned as grindstones or mills. This evolutionary strategy is seen in both ceratopsians and hadrosaurs, which became the absolute champions of chewing in the dinosaur world. But ornithischians also came up with less laborious solutions. In fact, the teeth of modern herbivores tend to be enormous, broad, and with at least one cutting part, so they can function as perfect vegetable choppers. Rhinoceros teeth are massive forms with sharpened edges. Certain ornithischians opted for a similar solution: for example, the teeth of stegosaurs or ankylosaurs,

while not as effective as those of a modern rhinoceros, were quite robust and equipped with dentated edges for cutting plants.

Some dinosaurs had modified tooth structures we might even call futuristic. *Heterodontosaurus* and its relatives, in fact, had teeth almost like mammals, with precanine teeth (similar to our incisors), canine teeth, and postcanine teeth (similar to our molars): a complete set for tearing and chewing vegetation.

Continue the adventure in volume 6,
T. Rex and the Great Extinction.

GLOSSARY

Angiosperms: flowering plants; a class of plants with the seeds enclosed in an ovary, which in many plants develops into an edible fruit or nut.

Benthos: the community of organisms that live on the seabed.

Conifers: plants without true flowers that develop their seeds in a cone, such as our pines and firs; often called "gymnosperms," which means "naked seed" and indicates that the seed is not enclosed in an ovary (compare to angiosperms).

Cosmopolitan: living throughout the entire world, describing an organism not restricted to a defined area or range. A cosmopolitan organism is called a "cosmopolite."

Gall: a sort of plant "tumor," a swelling produced by the plant to defend itself from intrusions, such as insect eggs or larvae.

Paleobiology: the study of the biology of organisms that exist only in the fossil record.

Sedimentation thrust of continental origin: a massive buildup of sediments that have originated in continental rather than marine environments; for example, terrestrial clays, as opposed to marine carbonates.

Systematics: the science that studies the interrelationships among living organisms.

Trophic niche: the ecological role of an organism within the community; its place within the food web.

DINOSAURS

1 THE JOURNEY: *Plateosaurus*

We follow the path of a great herd of *Plateosaurus* from the sea—populated by ichthyosaurs—through the desert and mountains, to their nesting places. Their trek takes place beneath skies plied by the pterosaur *Eudimorphodon*, and under the watchful eye of the predator *Liliensternus*.

We discover what life was like on our planet during the Triassic period, and how the dinosaurs evolved.

2 A JURASSIC MYSTERY: *Archaeopteryx*

What killed the colorfully plumed *Archaeopteryx*? Against the backdrop of a great tropical storm, we search for the perpetrator among the animals that populate a Jurassic lagoon, such as the small carnivore *Juravenator*, the pterosaur *Pterodactylus*, crocodiles, and prehistoric fish.

We discover how dinosaurs spread throughout the world in the Jurassic period and learned to fly, and how a paleontologist interprets fossils.

3 THE HUNTING PACK: *Allosaurus*

We see how life unfolds in a herd of *Allosaurus* led by an enormous and ancient male, as they hunt *Camarasaurus* and the armored *Stegosaurus* in groups, look after their young, and struggle amongst themselves. A young and powerful *Allosaurus* forces its way into the old leader's harem. How will the confrontation end?

We discover one of the most spectacular ecosystems in the history of the Earth: the Morrison Formation in North America.

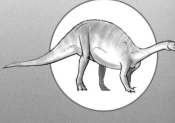